Lost in the Gardens

by J.H. Low

mc Marshall Cavendish
Children

To Xinni, Karen, Joyce & Mo

It was a day like no other!
For this was the day,
the day that Mom and Mei
were going to Gardens by the Bay.

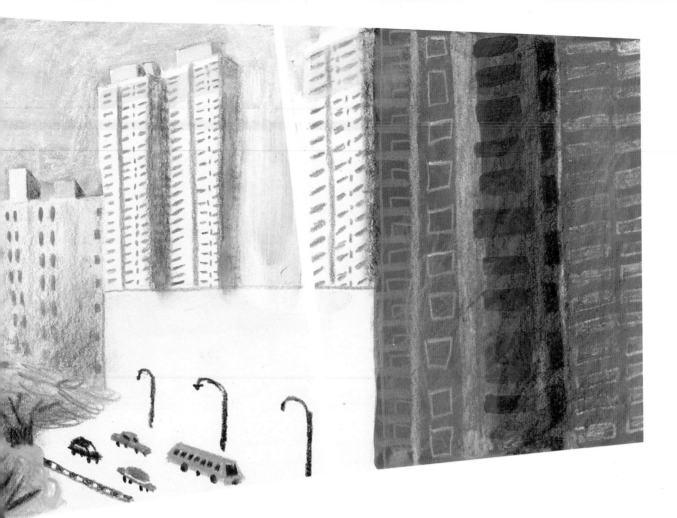

Away they went, off to Gardens by the Bay,
in a speedy MRT train.

"Where is Gardens by the Bay, Mom?"
asked the very excited Mei.

"Is it far, Mom? Why is it taking so long, Mom?
Are we near yet, Mom?"

"You will know soon Mei, you will know soon,"
smiled Mom.

Arrive they did. It was really quick.
People were marching like ants
at Bayfront MRT Station.
Left! Right! Left! Right!
Left and right!

"Why are all these people
in a rush, Mom?" asked Mei.

But there was no answer.

"Mom?"

"Mom?!"
Mei ran and ran.

"Mom!
Mom!"
Mei ran
*and ran
and ran.*

"Mom!
Mom!
Mom!
Mom!
Mom!
Mom!"
Mei cried out helplessly.

Feeling scared and worried,
Mei tried to hurry.

But her legs felt
heavier
and *heavier*
as she began to wonder
if she was going
to be on her own
forever.

Suddenly, Mei found herself surrounded by clouds of icy mist.

"Woo... chilly!" squealed Mei with a shiver.
"Why is this place so freezing?"

"This place is wintry cold, so that mountain plants here
can flourish and grow," came a deep voice from behind.

Mei turned around a little shocked,
wondering who that might be!

It was Wise Wee the bear,
standing quietly behind little Mei.

"Now tell me, what are you doing here
all alone in the Cloud Forest?" asked Wise Wee.

"Mom and I were going to visit Gardens by the Bay,"
said Mei with a little sniff. "But I lost her earlier today!"

"Oh my! That's not fine," gasped Wise Wee.
"Quick! Follow me! We will find her in a jiffy!"

The Cloud Forest was truly mysterious,
like the lost worlds in the movies.
Mei and Wise Wee looked to their
left and then to their right.
But Mom was nowhere in sight.

"Maybe Mom is not in the Cloud Forest,"
said Wise Wee. "Let's look somewhere else."

To the bustling Kingfisher Lake they went.

Wonderful creatures big and small.

Some short, some long, some very tall.

Mei had never seen anything like this.

She looked all around.

But Mom was nowhere in sight.

To the towering Supertree Grove they went.

"Wow! These must be the biggest trees
in the whole wide world," gushed Mei in awe.

It would be hard to find even a mammoth
in these trees. So Mei and Wise Wee
took care to turn every twig and leaf.
But Mom was nowhere in sight.

To the heavenly Flower Dome they went.

There were more flowers here than stars in the sky.

Red, blue, yellow, pink and white.

But Mom was nowhere in sight.

"Don't sigh, little Mei," said Wise Wee.

"Maybe at the Sun Pavilion your Mom we'll find."

To the desert-like Sun Pavilion they went.
The trees there looked the strangest —
spiky and dangerous. Threatening almost!

"Be careful now, mind the thorns,"
warned Wise Wee.

But Mei was not listening.
She was too busy searching for Mom.
As before, Mom was nowhere in sight.

"Let's expand our search,"
suggested Wise Wee.

So, Mei and the Wise Wee went plodding
along the bay, feeling a little dismayed.
They went as far as the Bay East Garden
and all the way back.
But Mom was still nowhere in sight.

"Can we take a break?" panted Mei,
who was rather tired by then.
"I am not used to so much walking."

"Yes, I could do with a little rest too,"
said Wise Wee.

They sat down on a log,
feeling a little short of breath.

"Could Mom also be looking for you?"
asked Wise Wee out of the blue.

"Oh yes! Why didn't I think of that?"
Mei nodded her head furiously.
"Hmm... so where might she be?"

"I know! Mom must be at the Children's Garden!"
exclaimed Wise Wee.

To the adventure-filled Children's Garden they went.
Mei never knew there could be so many fun things to do.
All the children were happy and engrossed in play.

"This must be the coolest place on earth!"
thought Mei.

For a moment, Mei forgot
about searching for Mom.
She and Wise Wee were too busy
splashing water and having fun.

Just then, Mei felt a pair of hands
cover her eyes from behind.
She knew those hands ever so well.
Mei turned around and shouted,
"Mom!"

Mom lifted Mei up
for a supersize hug,
and kissed her face
like she was never
going to stop.

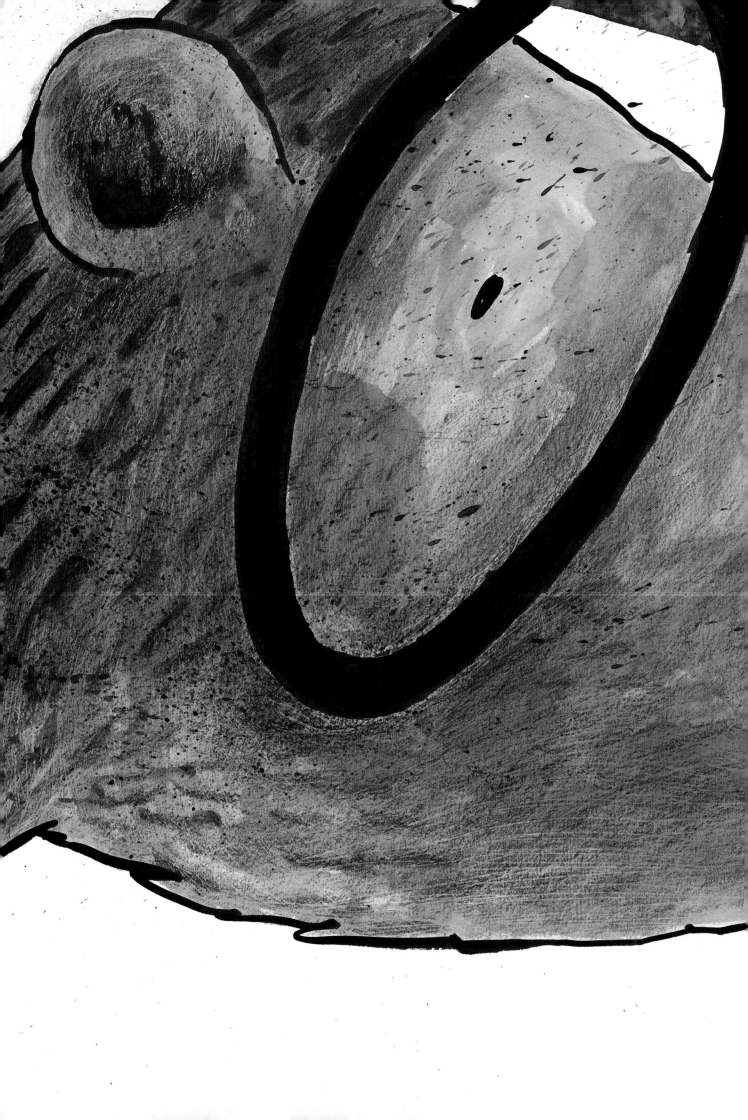

"Thank you for helping me find Mom,"
said Mei, kissing Wise Wee on his nose.

"There's nothing to it," smiled Wise Wee.
"Today has been very sweet."

Mom and Mei waved goodbye to Wise Wee
as they watched him slowly disappear
into the distant mist.

"Well then, shall we start
our tour of the Gardens?"
asked Mom.

"I am tired, Mom," said Mei,
as she rubbed her little eyes.
"Can we go home?"

Oh what a memorable day,
at Gardens by the Bay.

About the Author and Illustrator

J.H. Low has always been a passionate artist, illustrator and creator of stories. He holds a BA (Honours) in Fine Arts from the University of Leeds, UK, and an MA in Children's Books Illustration from the Anglia Ruskin University, UK. He received Honourable Mention for the prestigious MacMillan Prize 2009 for his book, *There is No Steak Buried Here*, which was translated into Chinese and became his first published book.

J.H.'s illustrations are spontaneous and masterful, and often imbued with a light touch of humour. He is the illustrator of *Dragon's Egg* (2012) by award-winning author, Carolyn Goodwin.

The book is also available as an app. *Lost in the Gardens* is J.H.'s first English language publication.

Published by Marshall Cavendish Children
An imprint of Marshall Cavendish International

Other Marshall Cavendish Offices:
Marshall Cavendish Corporation. 99 White Plains Road, Tarrytown NY 10591-9001, USA •
Marshall Cavendish International (Thailand) Co Ltd. 253 Asoke, 12th Flr, Sukhumvit 21 Road,
Klongtoey Nua, Wattana, Bangkok 10110, Thailand • Marshall Cavendish (Malaysia) Sdn Bhd,
Times Subang, Lot 46, Subang Hi-Tech Industrial Park, Batu Tiga, 40000 Shah Alam, Selangor
Darul Ehsan, Malaysia.

Marshall Cavendish is a trademark of Times Publishing Limited

National Library Board, Singapore Cataloguing-in-Publication Data
Low, Joo Hong, author.
Lost in the Gardens / by J.H. Low. – Singapore : Marshall Cavendish Children, [2015]
pages cm
ISBN : 978-981-4677-10-3
1. Gardens – Singapore – Juvenile fiction. 2. Parks – Singapore – Juvenile
fiction. 3. Mothers and daughters – Juvenile fiction. I. Title.
PZ7
428.6 -- dc23   OCN906658338

Printed by Times Offset (M) Sdn Bhd